Fletcher
and the
Falling Leaves

BY JULIA RAWLINSON
PICTURES BY TIPHANIE BEEKE

GREENWILLOW BOOKS, AN IMPRINT OF HARPERCOLLINSPUBLISHERS

The world was changing. Each morning, when Fletcher bounded out of the den, everything seemed just a little bit different. The rich green of the forest was turning to a dusty gold, and the soft, swishing sound of summer was fading to a crinkly whisper. Fletcher's favorite tree looked dull, dry, and brown.

Fletcher was beginning to get worried.

"I think my tree is sick," said Fletcher.

"What's wrong with it?" his mother asked.

"Its leaves are turning brown," said Fletcher.

"Don't worry, it's only autumn," she said.

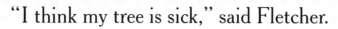

Fletcher ran back to his tree
and patted the rough bark.
"Don't worry, it's only autumn," he said.
"You'll be feeling better soon."

But the tree didn't get better. Each day,
more leaves turned brown. One morning
the wind blew a small brown leaf off of a
branch. Fletcher jumped up and caught it,
very gently, in his paw.

"Don't worry, tree. I've got your leaf.
I'll fix you." Fletcher looked around,
picked a piece of grass, and carefully
tied the leaf to a branch.

Just then another
gust of wind ruffled
Fletcher's fur. The
little leaf shook itself
free and fluttered
back to the ground.

Fletcher picked it up again and thought
very hard. Then he poked the leaf onto
a twig and pushed it down firmly.
"Now you hold on tight," said Fletcher.
"No more flying around."
The little leaf gave a tiny rustle in reply.

The next day, a strong wind was blowing through the forest. Fletcher rushed out of the den and ran all the way to his tree. Lots of branches were bare, and little lost leaves spun everywhere.

"Don't worry, tree. I'll catch them for you. I promise."

Round and round and round whirled Fletcher after the swirling leaves.

"Leaves! Wonderful! Just what I need
for my nest," said a squirrel.
"But these belong to the tree," said Fletcher.
"Don't take them away."
"The tree doesn't need them anymore," said the squirrel,
bounding off.
"Help! Help! The wind and the squirrel are stealing
our leaves," cried Fletcher.

"Leaves! Terrific! Just what I need to keep warm," said a porcupine,
   rolling around.

"But these belong to the tree," said Fletcher, plucking leaves
   from the porcupine's needles.
"Not anymore," snuffled the porcupine, and away he rolled.
"Help! Help! The wind, the squirrel, and the porcupine are stealing
   our leaves," cried Fletcher.

Suddenly a flock of friendly birds swooped down from the sky. They picked up the leaves in their beaks and poked them onto the tree's branches. Soon the tree was leafy again, and Fletcher flopped down and smiled.

"Thank you, birds, thank you," he gasped as the birds fluttered away. He lay looking up through the leaves at the sky, and drifted off to sleep.

But the wind continued to blow, and the branches still danced.

The leaves shivered and shook themselves and began to wriggle free.

They tossed and turned

and twitched and twirled

and tumbled to the ground.

They brushed Fletcher's ears and nose

and filled his dreams with a whispering sound.

When Fletcher finally woke up, he couldn't believe his eyes. Instead of a roof of dancing leaves, all he could see were bare branches against the sky. "Oh, tree. I am so sorry," gulped Fletcher. "All your leaves are gone."

But then he saw, high in the branches, one small leaf still holding on.

"I won't let the wind steal that one,"
said Fletcher, and he began to climb.

He crawled along to the last leaf
and held it firmly onto its branch.

All day long the wind blew,
the branch bounced,
and Fletcher held tight.
"I'll stay with you, leaf,"
he said. "Don't worry."

But then, with a sudden whoosh of wind, the branch
bounced high. With a *plip!* the leaf let go and fluttered
like a little flag clutched in Fletcher's paw.

Fletcher looked sadly at the leaf he had promised to save.
He carried it carefully down the tree and back to the den.

He made a cozy little bed for it and gently tucked it in. But
all night long he could only think of his tree, all on its own.

At dawn Fletcher tiptoed outside. The wind had finally stopped
blowing, and the air was cold. The moon still hung in the clear sky
and pale stars glimmered.

As he came to his favorite tree, Fletcher saw a magical sight . . .

The tree was hung with a thousand icicles, shining silver in the early light. "You are more beautiful than ever," whispered Fletcher. "But are you all right?"

A tiny breeze shivered the branches, making a sound like laughter, and in the light of the rising sun, the sparkling branches nodded.

Fletcher gave his tree a hug. Then he went back to the den for a nice, warm breakfast.

For Ben and Tom, with love—J. R.

For little John and Pauline, with love—T. B.

HarperTrophy® is a registered trademark of HarperCollins Publishers.

Fletcher and the Falling Leaves. Text copyright © 2006 by Julia Rawlinson.
Illustrations copyright © 2006 by Tiphanie Beeke.
First published in 2006 in Great Britain by Gullane Children's Books as *Ferdie
and the Falling Leaves*. First published in 2006 in the United States by Greenwillow Books.

The right of Julia Rawlinson to be identified as the author and Tiphanie Beeke
as the illustrator of this work has been asserted by them.
All rights reserved. Manufactured in China.
www.harpercollinschildrens.com

Pastels were used to prepare the full-color art. The text type is Glouces Old Style.

Library of Congress Cataloging-in-Publication Data
Rawlinson, Julia. Fletcher and the falling leaves / by Julia Rawlinson; pictures by Tiphanie Beeke.
p. cm.
"Greenwillow Books."
Summary: When his favorite tree begins to lose its leaves, Fletcher the fox worries that it is sick,
but instead a magical sight is in store for him.
ISBN: 978-0-06-113401-2 (trade bdg.) ISBN: 978-0-06-157397-2 (pbk.)
[1. Foxes—Fiction. 2. Trees—Fiction. 3. Leaves—Fiction.] I. Beeke, Tiphanie, ill.
II. Title. PZ7.R1974Fle 2006 [E]—dc22 2005034348

15 16 GBUK 10 9 8 7

Don't miss these other stories about Fletcher!

Fletcher and the Springtime Blossoms

Fletcher and the Snowflake Christmas